AFFINITY

The Tiny Girl with the Heart-Shaped Nose

Written by

BRENDALYN J

MYND
MATTERS

To purchase books in bulk or for additional information, contact the publisher.

Mynd Matters Publishing
715 Peachtree Street NE
Suites 100 & 200
Atlanta, GA 30308
www.myndmatterspublishing.com

ISBN: 978-1-957092-61-4 (pbk)
ISBN: 978-1-957092-62-1 (hdcv)

FIRST EDITION

To my grandchildren, Ava and Chase,
While Ava was only one when I wrote this book, Chase was in
kindergarten and inspired me to write this story.

It is my hope that both your stories in life turn out to be just as
successful as Affinity, aka Heart Girl. Remember always to give it
your best because…Enough is never enough.

There will always be a need to keep learning.

Contents

Chapter 1

Meet Affinity

My name is Affinity Ava Marshall, but you can call me HG. My dad gave me that nickname. You will find out how I got it later. I am very tiny for my age and have a unique-shaped nose. It looks like a little heart. It doesn't bother me that it's different (well, not anymore). People are all different in one way or another. Some people like being different. Some don't. I have learned to embrace my differences and not let them stop me from becoming who I can really be.

I attend Sperry-Elm School, where I am one of the two finalists in this year's spelling bee. Tomorrow is the big day, and I am so excited. I have studied and practiced for weeks preparing for this big event. Who would have ever thought that tiny me would have reached a milestone this big? I thought I never ever wanted to learn how to make words from sounds using what teachers call "phonics."

But here I am. Not only am I using phonics, I am also spelling words most kids my age can't even pronounce. I guess it is true what they say; having the will, determination, and lots of practice will take you many places. You just have to give learning a chance, no matter the subject.

As much as I thought reading was too hard, I knew it was something I would have to learn sooner or later. I decided to stop fighting myself about it and to just do it. I am glad I did. Mrs. Boyd, my favorite teacher, told me I am one of the best readers she has ever had in her classes. It made me feel good to hear that coming from her.

Not only have I gotten very good at phonics, but I can also spell little words, big words, and sometimes, gigantic words. I had convinced myself that learning to read was just too hard. Sometimes, it didn't seem to matter how hard I tried; I just could not make the connection between making sounds and creating words out of them. I had convinced myself I was a dummy when it came to reading. I knew that wasn't true, but telling myself that gave me a reason to avoid trying.

I love visiting my granny's house. As soon as I could walk, she would take me out to the yard, which was nothing more than a block of concrete, shared by some adjoining neighbors. We played kickball, softball, and basketball, and I played putt-putt golf with the miniature set she got for me. She didn't like playing golf, except on her Wii game. She still has the game, although I don't think she plays with it anymore.

Sometimes, she sat outside the open garage and rocked in her chair while I played. Playing with slime and blowing bubbles was a thing for me. She blew them, and I'd try to catch them. She would say, "I'm getting too old for this stuff." She still played with me anyway, unless she wasn't up to it on a particular day.

She bought me a training bike, a kid's motorcycle, all kinds of car toys, a learning globe, and a kid's computer, which I used to download games. Little did I know, the games were teaching me as well. And yes, she bought books too. There were no other kids in the neighborhood to play with, so she did her best to entertain me.

She was a good granny. At bedtime, we would take turns telling stories. Most of the time, we made them up as we went along. She said all my stories were about the wolf in the woods. She was right. That was because of the Red Robinhood story I had watched on video at school – my kindergarten teacher would let her class watch movies on Fridays after naptime. Making up stories with my grandmother was fun too.

At the time, I attended a Christian-based private school. I would tell Granny about the Bible stories we watched on video. She was always amazed at how I remembered the stories and their main characters. She would say, "I can tell you're paying attention." I did like watching movies at school, but not when they were scary.

One day at soccer practice, I didn't see my mom. Unknowingly, she had gone to talk with one of her coworkers at one of the other fields. Without any reason known to my granny, I began to misbehave…badly. After a while, my mother returned to where my granny was sitting. By then, Granny had become more than a little upset at my behavior. She said to my mom, "You need to take Affinity home. She won't listen to the coach and keeps playing inside the goal net." The next time I spent the weekend at Granny's house, she asked about my behavior at the soccer field. She was surprised at my response.

"It was that movie," I replied.

"What movie?" she asked.

"The one about Hansel and Gretel. The old lady, who looked like a witch, tricked them because she wanted to eat them for dinner. But they got away after Gretel pushed her into the hot oven. I didn't like that movie."

Granny understood what had happened. I started to misbehave when I couldn't see my mother and thought something must have happened to her. The next day, Granny visited my school and spoke to the lady in the front office about my experience. We didn't watch a movie the following Friday. The teacher let us have free play in the classroom. We still had movie time, but they were not scary like the Hansel and Gretel one. I do believe many books are based on something true. But I hope that book was based on somebody's bad dream, not real people.

My granny didn't want me to think all movies were bad like that one, so she started buying books for me. She was anxious for me to learn to read. She didn't like it when I said, "I'm just dumb. I'm never gonna learn to read."

She'd say, "You're not dumb. You just need all the practice you can give yourself."

Practice meant words. "No, thanks."

She was by herself with that thought. Her reading books to me was enough while I looked at pictures. That was all I needed to understand the story.

If the book had rhyming sentences, she'd read each one up to the last word. She would then pause, waiting for me to finish the sentence. I enjoyed that, but it still did not inspire my interest in reading without her. But I really liked being at her house because she let me have fun most of the time. Somedays, it was like I was in school. She would interrupt me from playing and say, "HG, let's sound out some words."

I'd just say, "We can do that later." Then she would try to negotiate by telling me that if I did just a few small words, we could play afterward. Sometimes I gave in. Other times I cried. Didn't she know all kids wanted to do was play? Besides, I had a long time before I needed to know how to read.

My grandmother was a good reader. She knew how to make words by sounding out letters. She said her class had a spelling bee when she was in the fifth grade. She won, and the teacher gave her one of those round chocolate-covered candies filled with coconut. She talked about that like it was a huge deal to her.

I had convinced myself that sounding out words was too hard. I much preferred working with numbers, not words. There was something exciting about adding and subtracting. When Granny would say, "Let's do some numbers," I was all in! She was happy that I liked math, but Granny refused to give up on my learning to read. Her determination paid off. I finally began to connect the dots. Before I knew it, I was sounding out letters and saying real words. When I would say a word correctly, Granny would clap her hands and say, "You did it! Now, give me a big hug. I really did like getting those grandmother hugs.

I liked watching learning shows for kids on television. Sometimes my granny would watch with me. But she didn't enjoy watching shows with critters and snakes in them. She always said,

"I hate bugs, and I'm scared of snakes."

One day when she opened her front door, after I rang the doorbell, I threw a rubber snake at her. You would have thought it was real the way she jumped and screamed. I laughed. She was so funny. I picked it back up and said, "Look, Granny, this snake ain't real."

She looked at me and said, "It looked real to me."

One time, my aunt was visiting, and we talked about jellyfish. I don't remember why we were on that subject. But I do remember my granny asking how jellyfish caught their prey. Confidently, I answered, "Cnidocytes." I was only five at the time, so they were astonished. My aunt said, "That's a big word. How do you know that?"

They didn't believe that was the correct answer, so my aunt looked it up on her cell phone. Then she said, "She's right!"

None of us knew how to spell it. It was a big word for a little kid to remember. Since then, I have learned how it is spelled, of course, with help from the internet. My granny told me I was smart for my age but couldn't understand why I disliked reading.

Not only was Granny trying to teach me to read, but she also tried to make me out to be an artist. She'd grab an art canvas, paintbrushes, and paint. Then, she would back her car out of the garage so we could sit on the concrete floor and paint. Granny always praised me for my paintings. After I had finished my painting, I had to name it. I called my first one "Squibble." The next time I visited her, I saw Squibble hanging on the wall. After a few more painting sessions, she had a collection of my paintings hanging on walls in her office, which was also my playroom. She told me, "One day, you are gonna be a famous artist."

Looking back, I know what my granny was doing. She wasn't just trying to entertain me. She was my personal coach but in a loving and fun way. She was guiding me so I could figure out on my own which activity I felt most happy doing. Back then, it definitely was not reading. In fact, that was the one thing I liked doing the least. But this story is not about my love for math, art, or science. It is about what happened when I changed my perspective on reading.

One day when I was visiting Granny, she became frustrated with me. I'd never seen her get upset because I didn't want to practice reading. She said, "Okay then, if you don't want to learn, then go play. See how far that gets you in life."

As I got older, the nighttime stories between us happened less. Granny must have been trying to figure out how she could motivate me to read. I could tell she did not want me to get discouraged and give up on reading altogether. She decided to read to me more. After each reading, she would say, "Now, what was that story all about? What or who was the book about?" She would ask how the story made me feel: happy, sad, or scared. That was just my granny's way of making me think. I do admit, I fought against her attempts for a long time. However, in the end, she influenced me more than she could ever know.

Chapter 2

A Greater Influence

I attended middle school and began to read more. Although my granny had significantly impacted me, my biggest motivation for reading came from the new girl at our school, Kaaya Madison. I knew when I first saw Kaaya we would quickly become friends. She didn't act like most of the other girls in my class. She was friendly and always wore a smile. Let me tell you all about our story.

Not once did I see Kaaya get angry at anyone or look sad about anything, even though some of the other kids made fun of her for no reason. I think they were jealous because Mrs. Boyd immediately took a liking to Kaaya. Behind her back, they would say she was the teacher's favorite and called her "The Pet."

Each Friday afternoon, while we had snack time, Mrs. Boyd would have a student give a presentation to the class. Sometimes she decided on the topic the student would present. Other times, she would allow the student to choose their own presentation. Some students shared experiences about their family events; others did show and tell. I never volunteered.

Kaaya loved presenting. She had no fear of standing in front of the class and talking about books she had read or was reading. Immediately, I could tell she had a love for books. After a few of her presentations, it was like we had our own classroom storyteller. Kaaya came to our school after we returned from Christmas break. When Mrs. Boyd introduced her to the class, she told us Kaaya had learned to read when she was only three. Only three? How was it even possible that a three-year-old could learn to read at all? It had to be hard leaving all of her friends and coming to a new school where she didn't know anybody. But Kaaya was friendly. She had no problem making new friends.

When the teacher called her to the front of the room, she would confidently smile and share the story from the book she had chosen for the week. Kaaya read portions of it out loud and would end with her interpretation of the story. Sometimes, she would even change her voice to sound like some of the characters she was reading about. Other times, she would do a solo skit as part of her presentation. She would ask for volunteers when she needed assistance. It was like she was acting in a play. She was very dramatic in her storytelling, so we looked forward to her presentation days.

I could tell she loved to read; she always picked the kind of books that made you want to pay attention and listen. At the end of her story, she would say, "Now the moral of this story is…" She would then finish with her interpretation of what the author wanted the reader to know. The thought often crossed my mind that there was something different about her and that she would be a very important person one day. Doing what? I had not decided yet. A teacher? Maybe. Public speaker? Maybe. All I know is I enjoyed listening to Kaaya tell her stories.

And then I had this weird thought that maybe, just maybe, Kaaya was an angel in disguise sent to our school on a mission, especially for me. My mom often told me, "Be careful who you are talking to. That person just might be an angel sent to present you with a special message."

Well, if that is true, I wondered what message Kaaya was sent to give me. It soon crossed my mind that if Kaaya could be a storyteller, so can I. So, I began to read books with very few words on the page. As the words became easier to read, I read books with more words. I realized reading was not so bad after all. Before I knew it, I was standing in front of the class, telling stories about books I had read. Even my mom noticed my growing interest in books. When we would visit a store like Target or Walmart, she would allow me to peruse the book section while she shopped.

One day, I came home from school to five new books my mom had purchased for me to read. They were about Black people who had made a difference in our country. One of the books was about Harriet Tubman, the lady they called "Moses." She helped a lot of people run away from slavery. In school, I learned it was called "The Underground Railroad." Another book was about a man named Dr. Martin Luther King, Jr. He was instrumental in helping people receive the right to vote.

There was a book on Rosa Parks. She refused to give up her seat to a White man on the bus, so she went to jail. You see, Black people had to sit at the back of the bus back then. They were not allowed to drink water from the same fountain or use the same restroom as White people. And that's not even getting close to the history of the Black people who suffered after involuntarily crossing from Africa to this country to work for free. Those who tried to escape were often caught, beaten, or killed. It's horrible that one human being would be so cruel to another.

One of the books was about a man whose father was from Africa who became our country's first Black president. His name is Barack Obama. I know you're thinking, "She can't be that good in math. That's only four books."

You would be correct. The fifth one was about a carved piece of wood titled *The Adventures of Pinocchio*. The book was written in the 1800s by a man named Carlo Collodi. My grandmother read it to my mother when she was a child. She said the book clearly showed how bad things continue to follow people who are selfish, mischievous, and dishonest, but that a change in perspective and behavior could also bring about good.

I read all five. They are now part of the collection I keep in the little book closet my mom made for me. She made it by purchasing wood from a nearby store and gluing the pieces together. She added a design to it and called it *Affinity's Peek-in-a-Book* box. It was like I had my very own library in my bedroom. I was beginning to enjoy reading, even those little books you get when you buy a kid's meal at a fast-food restaurant. I keep quite a few of those in my little library. Books are books, and I always learn something when I read them. As Granny used to say, "Every book has a story to be told, and every story has a moral value to be learned."

Chapter 3

Little Teach

Back to the beginning. One day, I was walking down the halls at school, not looking where I was going. Suddenly, I turned and bumped into Kaaya, knocking her down to the floor. "Kaaya, I'm so sorry! I wasn't looking where I was going. I'm so very sorry," I repeated.

As I helped her stand back up, she said, "I'm okay. I know you didn't do that on purpose. Next time, just be careful and watch where you're going. You wouldn't want to hurt anybody. Would you?"

"No! Not at all," I responded. I asked where she was headed. "To the cafeteria," she replied. Eager to join her, I responded, "Me too." So, we walked through the halls and then ate lunch together. That was the beginning of our friendship.

Kaaya was not shy at all. In fact, she was very outspoken. But she was nice. After that, we ate lunch together every day. Before long, we had become like two peas in a pod. Sometimes, we would have sleepovers at my house, other times at hers.

The first time I visited Kaaya, she showed me her bedroom.

There were books everywhere. I could tell her mom liked books too because their home had several book cabinets. Her mom was very nice, but I never saw her dad.

I had noticed a man's picture on her dresser. I inquired if he was her dad. She sadly said, "Yes," and then told me he had been killed while they were living in another country. Both her mom and dad had been in the Army. Kaaya told me she was adopted and was an only child. She had always wanted a little sister or brother. I told her I wasn't adopted but was an only child. She asked me if I had ever wanted a sister or brother.

"Sometimes I wish I had a sister, but not a brother," I responded.

"Why?" she asked.

"Because boys get in trouble too much," I said.

She then asked if I wanted to be her pinky-sister.

"Pinky-sister? What is that?" I curiously asked.

"It's when two girls don't have the same mom and dad but agree to be sisters by locking their pinky fingers together and saying the magic words."

"What magic words?"

"Pinky-sisters for life."

And that is how Kaaya and I became both besties and sisters. As we lay horizontally across the bed with our feet dangling on the side, we talked and giggled about the boys in our class. We found out we each liked one of the Singleton twins. She thought Chip was the cutest. I liked Chaz. Afterward, we played games on my phone, watched a movie, and then drifted off to sleep.

Some parents don't agree with their children having a cell

phone. My mom was different. She had given me one in case of an emergency and made it clear how to use it. I could not visit certain websites on the internet, and I had to turn it off once I got home from school. Otherwise, I was only allowed to have it while away from home.

I obeyed my mom because I never wanted her to take it away from me. It made me feel like I was somebody important. I guess to my mom, I was. Besides, it was also a way for her to know my whereabouts at any time. I didn't mind. It mattered a lot that my mom took this precaution for my safety.

Hanging with Kaaya was never not fun. She always wanted to do this one thing when we had sleepovers. We had to play a game that involved learning new words. So, she came up with a creative spelling bee game.

Sometimes, she would hold up a card for me to pronounce the word, meaning I had to listen very carefully for the sound of each letter. She would pronounce a word for me to spell, sometimes intentionally not sounding it out very clearly. That was her way of forcing me to ask her to repeat the word.

I then understood why Kaaya was so good at reading. At first, it felt like we were doing schoolwork, and I didn't want to be in school at our sleepovers. What kid wanted to learn when they could be playing? Of course, that would be my bestie, Kaaya. Believe it or not, she was beginning to rub off on me.

Amazingly, this game turned out to be very useful in helping me recognize why I had a hard time learning to read.

First, she said, "Stop getting so frustrated; that's why you give up so easily." Then she would say, "Take a deep breath. It helps to relax and keep calm."

"How did you get so smart?" I asked.

"My mom and spelling coach. But of course, I read a lot too."

I wasn't sure if she had actually been in a spelling bee, so I asked.

"I sure was, and I won the championship for two years straight," she shared proudly.

"I wanna be in a spelling bee," I said excitedly.

"Really?" Then Kaaya gave me some kid-glove words of advice. She simply said, "You can. But you can't let fear keep you from trying. With some initiative, dedication, commitment, and a whole lot of practice, you just might be surprised by your own success."

Chapter 4

Book Box Challenge

One weekend, Kaaya spent a Saturday night at my house. We were on my phone watching a little girl close to our age being interviewed by a popular television talk-show host. She was between seven and eight years old. What made her interview go viral on the internet was not just that she was so young, but she had read and then given away over 2,000 books for others to read. As we watched the video, the little girl reminded me of Kaaya with her love for reading and helping others learn to read as well. Although I had begun to read more myself and enjoyed new books here and there, I thought that might be way too much of my time spent with books.

As the young girl continued to tell her story, she spoke about the day her dad surprised her with a small book box he had made for her. It had a glass lift-top door that could be opened to retrieve the books. The little girl loved it so much that she came up with an idea. She put it at the edge of the sidewalk near their front yard. Then she placed a sign on it that read: "Take one. Reading is Fun-and-Mental."

Each day she would see fewer books in the box. By the end of the second week, all but three of the books had been taken. She began to wonder if her books were actually being read or if someone was taking them out of the box just to be mean. One day, she decided to watch the box from her bedroom window to see if anyone had stopped by to get a book. To her surprise, a van stopped in front of the house. She noticed a little girl and an older-looking boy exit the van and approach the box.

To her amazement, they were perusing through the books. She couldn't tell how many, but she saw them walk back to their van with some books in their hands. She was so elated that children were taking books. At that moment, she became even more excited. She thought, "I have to put some more books in the box." She called family members and visited neighbors' houses, asking for any children's books they no longer wanted. Before she knew it, her family's garage was filled with books. Befuddled by the sight of many, she remarked to her dad, "Oh, my goodness! Daddy, what am I going to do with all these books? I didn't expect to get this many. I don't have but one book box. How am I going to give them all away?"

"Well," responded her dad, "You asked for this. But don't worry your little head off. There is something I can do to help."

"What's that, Daddy?" Her dad worked in construction and loved working with wood. He told her, "I will build you some more book boxes. We'll have to obtain permission from the city before we can place them around town. In addition to the one outside our house, I'll make five more. As people take a book, they can leave one, but only if they want to. That will help to keep the book box filled up." So, her dad built the boxes, and the little girl and her mom painted beautiful designs on them. Before long, the little girl had started something new and big in her own city.

Since Kaaya and I became friends, everything seemed to be about reading. After the video ended, I said to Kaaya, "That's so awesome! Because of her, other kids can read more books." Out of nowhere, Kaaya said, "You should join the upcoming spring spelling bee team. I think you will do great."

"Me?" I said, doubting myself.

Looking around the room, she said, "Who else would I be talking to?"

Not wanting to compete against the best reader I knew, I asked, "What about you? Are you going to sign up?"

Without a flinch, she replied. "Nope. I want you to join. I wouldn't want to compete against my best friend." Laughing at her own self, she said, "Besides, you know I would win."

I could only respond, "You're probably right."

That was the beginning of Kaaya's "Call-to-Challenge." She continued, "It'll be hard, but it can also be lots of fun, especially if you are the final winner."

"I dunno, Kaaya. Some words can be very hard to pronounce. Trying to spell them can be even harder," I grumbled.

"HG, don't worry. You'll get a practice list of words to study. If you commit to studying them every day, trust me, you will do just fine. You know I am here to help.

After pondering a few moments, I said, "Okay, I wanna do it." Kaaya had put me to the challenge, and reluctantly, I accepted. I don't like standing in front of a big crowd of people. That's why I had been reluctant to give a Friday presentation in class. Standing on a stage with lots of people watching would be a huge deal. What had I gotten myself into?

A few days later, the announcement came out. Mrs. Boyd told us we would have a spelling bee to help her decide whose name to submit to represent the class. She asked for volunteers. Hands immediately began going up. After a few moments, they stopped.

Mrs. Boyd said, "That's only nine. I need one more volunteer."

I looked over at Kaaya, who was already looking at me. We both smiled, knowing what each other was thinking. Before I could change my mind, she grabbed my hand, stretching it up as high as she could get it. Once she realized I was going to keep it up, she let go.

"This is great," said Mrs. Boyd. "That's a good number to compete and to give some of you more practice with words." She went on to explain, "For our spelling bee, we will have a third-place prize, second-place prize, and a first-place winner, whose name I will submit to the Spring Spelling Bee committee. I only have two weeks before I will have to submit a name." She then handed each volunteer a list of words to study. I looked down at the page.

I held my hand to my mouth so my scream wouldn't come out too loud. "Oh, my goodness! These are some really big words." I heard laughter. Mrs. Boyd assured me and the other volunteers we would do well if we studied hard enough. The class spelling bee began the following Monday. At the end of week one, there were only three contestants left. The good thing about that was each of us would be a winner. It was only the size of the prize that made the difference.

Second and third-prize winners would get ribbons. The first-prize winner would get a small trophy from Mrs. Boyd and go on to represent our class at the Spring Spelling Bee. That was the prize I was really going for. At the end of week two, I won the prize – Kaaya helped me with my word list.

"Congratulations, Affinity. Great job! You know what that means," said Mrs. Boyd. Kaaya intervened. "Yes! She does. It means Affinity will represent us at the Spring Spelling Bee. I already know she is going to bring home the big trophy."

"That's the right attitude, Kaaya. What about you, Affinity? Do you believe you will be our new champion?" asked Mrs. Boyd.

"You bet I am!" I shouted as I held my little gold trophy high for everybody in the class to see.

The Spring Spelling Bee was set for May 1st, which was also my mom's birthday – another reason to win. It was now the middle of February, and I had just over two months to prepare. In addition to doing my class assignments, the word list became a part of my homework to ensure I studied them every day. My mom told me to rest on weekends so I would not burn myself out from so much study.

It was hard not to study when Kaaya and I had sleepovers. We would play our version of a spelling bee because I had to be ready when the time came. As the time drew closer, I became more comfortable and confident with the words on the list. Kaaya had learned how to research word origins during her previous spelling bees. She said, "Knowing the origin of a word could be very helpful, especially if you've never heard it before." She told me once I learned some of the tricks to spelling, I could practically spell any word.

She went on to say, "Listening carefully as a word is pronounced is very important. To spell a word correctly, you must hear every sound. And you have to decipher the syllables, prefixes, and suffixes. That's just the beginning. There are a whole lot of rules when learning to spell."

Having Kaaya as my friend was like having a teacher away from school. Was she a mini-size teacher? She sure did act like one. Or maybe she was my mission angel sent to guide me through this new adventure.

Chapter 5

Change

My mom is a writer and works from home. My dad is a well-known public school teacher at Woodbridge Elementary. He loved teaching. So, he was elated to be offered a position at DTIC Elementary. A few days later, my dad came home from work and told my mom and me there was something he needed to talk to us about. That evening we all gathered around the table and sat down to eat dinner. My mom had cooked my favorite, spaghetti. As if he didn't have anything to tell us, my dad sat down and began to eat his spaghetti. Mom and I looked at him, then at each other.

Simultaneously, we both nudged our shoulders. I had no idea what this was all about. By the expression on my mom's face, neither did she. Mom and I picked up our forks and began to eat our dinner, anticipating that Dad would soon put his fork down and start talking. He didn't. He kept us waiting.

After a few moments, I could tell Dad's non-verbal actions had gotten the best of Mom. She calmly asked, "Honey, why are you keeping us in the dark? What is it that you want to talk about?"

"Yeah, Dad. Stop making us wait. What is it you want to tell us?" Obviously, he was relishing his meal and wanted to finish eating his spaghetti. He looked up, realizing Mom and I had stopped eating and were waiting for him to say something, anything. After he laid his fork down on the plate, he finally said something. It was about time. Whatever he was going to say, he obviously had not talked to Mom first.

"I've been offered a new teaching position," he said in an undertone, almost as if he had been afraid to tell us. I was a little confused. That sounded like good news to me. "That's great, Daddy! What will you be teaching?"

"This is a once-in-a-lifetime opportunity, one to which I just could not say no," he said, sounding a little more cheerful about it.

I asked, "Why do you look so somber, Daddy?"

"Because it's at DTIC Elementary," he replied.

For some reason, Mom didn't seem all that happy about his news. She excused herself from the table and went into the kitchen for a few moments. Upon her return, she said, "That's great, Honey, I'm happy for you," as she took her seat again. Mom knew exactly where DTIC was located and what getting this new job meant for the family. Dad looked at mom with suspicion, possibly doubting sincerity in what she'd just said. It was apparent she was a little angry at him for not talking this over with her first.

At that moment, what else was there for him to say except, "Thank you, Dear." He added, "But there is something else we need to discuss."

"What's that, Daddy," I asked. I was not ready for the response I got.

"We will have to move to a new location, so I don't have a long commute to work."

His news did not sit too well with me, not at all. The excitement of hearing his so-called good news had just taken a downward turn for me. I could tell I wasn't alone in how I felt about the news Dad had just spilled on us; Mom's expression had grown dimmer.

Silence crept into the room as I sat there trying to muddle through what my dad had just said. If a pen had dropped, we could have heard it. The spaghetti smelled so good under my nose, but I had lost my appetite. I did not like the idea that I would soon have to leave my friends to attend a new school where I didn't know anybody. Tears began to drizzle down my face.

"What's wrong, Dear?" Mom said softly.

"My friends are here, and we always have fun together. I make good grades, and I have good teachers." At that moment, I thought about my teacher, Mrs. Boyd, and smiled. My mom smiled back, looking at me with curiosity. Audibly, I continued with my thoughts. "Sometimes Mrs. Boyd can be a hard teacher, but I know it's because she wants us to learn and do our best. She is the best teacher at the school."

"One day, I was walking through the hallways heading to the restroom when I overheard two teachers talking. I heard one say Mrs. Boyd's name. Then, I heard the other teacher say, 'I know. My nephew is in her class and said her name should be changed to Monster General.' The other teacher chuckled. I wanted to run and tell Mrs. Boyd what I had just heard, but I knew that would make her feel sad, probably angry, and I could get into trouble.

After that, I just wanted to punch those teachers as hard as I could whenever I saw them at school. I was scared. So, I decided that would not be good for me either."

"Well, I sure am happy you did the right thing. You had no idea what those teachers were talking about. You could have caused a big misunderstanding among all of them. Most of the time, it is best for children to leave grown-ups to their own business," chided Mom.

Seemingly, Dad was glad we had changed the subject. He chimed into the conversation. "Mom's right, Kiddo. Sometimes it's best to leave matters alone when they don't involve you."

"Yeah, I know. I still like my school. If I go to a new school, I won't know anybody, and Mrs. Boyd won't be there. Kaaya won't be there either. I won't have any friends at that new school. What if my new teacher is not-a nice person? I feel very sad just thinking about that. Dad, why do we have to move anyway? Why can't we stay in this house? Can't you drive to the new school like you do now?"

"Kiddo, that's a lot of questions! HG, Honey, I understand exactly how you feel. Dad doesn't want to move either. Your mom and I love it here. This will be a big adjustment for us too. We have made lots of friends in this neighborhood. We'll have to leave them too, and I will be leaving some of my close coworkers. Just because we might have to move doesn't mean we can't keep in touch with some of our closest friends. It's not like we are moving to another state. We can still see them, just not as often as we do now. Don't you agree, Dear," Dad prodded.

Before Mom could respond, I yelled out another question.

"Why you, Dad?" There are lots of teachers who can take the job. Why does it have to be you?" I asked angrily.

He replied, "One of their teachers didn't return after the Christmas holidays. I think it was because of the loss of a close relative. So, the position is vacant. For the time being, it is being filled by one of the paraprofessionals who work at the school. Honey, do you remember Mr. Akers, who used to work at my school?"

"Yes, I remember him. He and his wife came to our house for the dinner we hosted Christmas before last," Mom answered. "He left Woodbridge last year to become the Assistant Principal at DTIC Elementary."

"He recommended me for the job."

"So, when will you have to start?" asked Mom.

"Mr. Akers wants me to report in two weeks," replied Dad.

"Two weeks!" shouted Affinity.

"Yes. I know. That gives us very little time to find a house and move."

"I think you meant no time," Mom grumbled somewhat sarcastically.

"If anyone would understand, I thought it would be my wife. Two against one, I see," said Dad. "Okay, I can probably consider commuting, at least for the remainder of this year. We can move during the summer and be in our new house by next fall," he conceded, realizing it was only fair since he hadn't discussed it with our family before saying yes to the job offer.

"I like that thought. Then, we'll have more time to plan and organize the move. That makes me feel so much better about this," said Mom, as she pecked a kiss on his forehead. Dad had proudly won her over. Now, it was my turn.

"HG, you know I love what I do and am an excellent teacher. That school needs me, and I do want to help. DTIC is where it began for many young kids who have gone on to do important things in life."

Speaking nonchalantly, I asked, "What does DTIC stand for anyway?"

Excitedly, he replied, "It's an acronym for Discovering Talent, Initiative, and Comprehension. DTIC is all about excellence, and I'm an excellent teacher."

"Okaaay! Okaaay! I get it. And Dad, I agree. You are an excellent teacher, and I know you are doing what you think is best for the school and our family. But I still don't like that we will have to move. If we move during the summer, I won't have any old friends to hang out with, and I might not make any new ones until school starts in the fall." For a moment, I paused in thought, then continued, "This could be my worst summer yet. I do love you, Dad. If we must move, so be it. I guess I'm okay with that. If DTIC needs the best, then it needs you."

Feeling like a winner, Dad replied, "That's what I've been trying to say all along. I knew you would understand my little Heart Girl."

"I do. I just hope there are no bullies at that new school."

"Why do you say that, HG?" asked Dad.

"There is this boy at my school now who likes to call people ugly names. He calls me Alien-Girl. He is always picking on other kids and making them do not-so-nice things to the other kids."

"Sounds like your school has a bully," said Mom.

"At first, it bothered me that he called me that, but not anymore. I don't understand why he likes bullying people," I responded. Then Mom added her thoughts.

"You know Finni, sometimes bullies don't know why they behave the way they do. Maybe he doesn't like something about himself and bully others to hide his truth, giving him a false sense of control. You can bet he is hurting inside about something. Maybe in some way he feels inferior to others. Maybe he lives in fear or in a bad home environment.

"I mean, there are reasons on top of reasons that kids bully. For them, this act of aggression becomes a way of protecting themselves from feeling more hurt. If a person is not emotionally strong, they become easy targets for bullies. Maybe that is why it doesn't bother you anymore. You took control and refused to allow his bullying to make you feel unworthy of being you."

"Mom, that makes sense. Maybe I should not look at him as a bad person. I bet he just wants to be liked and have friends, just like the rest of us kids. For the time I have left at that school, I'm going to do my best to be kind to him. That's if he lets me."

"Sounds like you learned something from this experience," said Mom.

"I guess I did. God made us different for a reason, and He knows what it is. Sometimes people try to hide their feelings about themselves by criticizing and picking on others. We shouldn't make others feel bad so we can feel better about ourselves. Internally, that doesn't work anyway. And it's better to lift others up and not try to destroy them with ugly words.

Sometimes, we just need to get to know other people before judging them based on their appearance."

"That sounds like a great lesson learned, HG," Dad added. Changing the subject, he said, "Are we okay now? About the job, I mean."

What was there for me to say, I'm the kid in the family, so I just answered, "Yeah, Dad, we're good."

Changing the subject again, I said, "Come to think of it, Kaaya is different too. But it doesn't change anything about my being friends with her."

"How is Kaaya different?" asked Mom.

Acknowledging that I'd just recently learned about this, I said, "At our last sleepover, Kaaya told me she is hard of hearing in one of her ears. I noticed she would turn her right ear near the face of the person talking. Although I never asked why, I did think it was odd. I asked if her being partly deaf bothered her. She humbly said, 'No, I'm gifted in other ways.'"

Dad waited until I finished my story before chiming back in. "I need to grade some papers. Just want to make sure; we are good, HG?"

"Dad, why are you asking me again? I told you I was okay. After all, it's your decision to make. I can always make new friends. Besides, Kaaya and I both have Apple phones. We can Facetime each other anytime we wanna talk."

"That's my Finni," as they often affectionately called me. Dad left the room and went to his office to work.

"Affinity, I'm glad you are feeling better about Dad's new job," said Mom. "I am too. But for now, you have homework to complete. You need to get into bed early. Go!" Mom exclaimed, "Tomorrow is your big day!"

I said, "Okay, I'm going," and left her to do the dishes. Leaning my head in the doorway of his office, I told my dad good night.

"Goodnight, HG." Then I rushed to my bedroom, quickly finished my homework, took a bath, and decided what I would wear to school the next day. I took a pair of folded blue jeans from my dresser drawer.

Hmm, maybe not the jeans. I'm going to be on a stage in front of a lot of people. I voted against the pants and decided on my favorite purple dress.

It was still hard to believe. I, the tiny girl with the heart-shaped nose, would soon be standing on our school's auditorium stage, representing my class in tomorrow's Spring Spelling Bee. As I stood looking in the mirror, I said to the Affinity looking back at me, "You know, if you win tomorrow, that opens the door to compete on a national level." I looked back at the Affinity in the mirror, "You're right. Let's do this!" My excitement was getting to be too much, and I wasn't even at the spelling bee yet.

Standing there, I thought, "I'm glad Kaaya will not be competing against me. I don't mean to doubt myself, but she is good, really good. Instead, Robbie Mack is my competition. He might be the reigning spelling bee champion today, but there is a new champ in town, and my name is Affinity."

"Tomorrow, I'm gonna walk out on that stage and confidently accept my trophy. I can hear it now, 'And the new champion for this year's spelling bee is — drum roll, please. Affinity Marshall.'"

Settling down from my excitement, I laid the dress across the back of the chair, said a prayer, and crawled into bed. No sooner than my head hit the pillow, I was fast asleep. My mom usually comes into my room to say "good night" and turn out the light. If she did, I didn't hear a thing.

My Big Day Tomorrow!

Chapter 6

The Big Day

G ood morning, Affinity. Time to get up. Today is your big day." Hearing mom's voice, I opened my eyes and quickly jumped out of bed.

"Mom, what time is it?"

"Don't worry. You didn't oversleep. Now go get dressed. There's a big breakfast waiting for you in the kitchen. I think I might be more excited than you about the spelling bee today. I know you are going to do well, my little champion," she encouragingly said.

"Thanks, Mom!"

I felt nervousness coming to the surface again and questioned if I was ready to do this. As quickly as I had that thought, Angel Kaaya whispered in my ear, "Breathe, keep calm, and relax." As I entered the kitchen, I stopped and did just that – it helped. So, I finished breakfast, grabbed my backpack, and left to catch the bus.

As I got near the bus stop, I remembered I hadn't said goodbye to my mom. I turned to go back into the house. She was standing inside the doorway. As I walked towards her, she met me in the yard. She had tears in her eyes. I said, "Mom, why are you crying? Are you alright?"

"Yes, I'm fine, Finni. I am just so proud of you. For you, enough is never enough. You gave it your best, and that itself makes you a winner."

"Thanks, Mom!"

I hugged her and joined the other kids at the bus stop. She yelled out to me, "You got this!" I waved and got on the bus. I sat in my seat and continued to wave until she was out of sight.

After arriving at school and seated at my desk, I felt a nervousness creeping up on me. This was not the time to get nervous. The Spring Spelling Bee would be starting in less than an hour. Teachers had already begun to assemble their classes in the auditorium. The spelling bee coach had instructed me to remain behind the stage curtains until my name was called to be seated.

As I stood backstage, I heard lots of movement and chattering in the auditorium, so I peered from behind the curtains to see what was happening. "Oh, my goodness!" The auditorium was already filled with people. I swear I could hear my heart beating. I wasn't calm. I had to get that under control. I silently took another deep breath and told myself, "Whatever is going on out there, do not let it stress you." I peered through the curtains again.

Although she could not see me, I spotted my mom as she was escorted to her seat. Someone called my name. I turned to see the spelling bee coach telling me we were about to begin. The coach had given contestants a list of basic spelling rules. He said, "Knowing these rules can prove very helpful if you get stumped by a word you are unfamiliar with." While I waited backstage, I recited some of those rules in my head.

Robbie was called out onto the stage first. Then my name was called. As I was about to take my seat, I heard a familiar voice yell, "Hey, look! It's that girl with the funny-shaped nose!" I recognized the loud and obnoxious voice. It was Sonny Braxton, the school's bully. He only picked on girls. He was too afraid of the boys. He had once gotten into a fight with another boy for saying ugly things about the boy's sister, and he got a real beat down too.

I admit hearing those words said about me was a little humiliating. I immediately felt myself getting mad. I wanted to throw something and knock his little pea-brain out. Then, he wouldn't be able to say ugly things about people anymore. I know that was not a nice thought to have, but at that moment, I couldn't be held accountable for the way I was thinking.

I took back control of my thoughts and began to focus on my purpose for being there in the first place. I put a smile back on my face and sat down. Then, I spotted Kaaya sitting in the front row in the middle section. She gave me a big smile and a thumbs-up. I smiled back.

The moderator approached the podium and began speaking from the microphone. It surprised me that Mrs. Boyd was the spelling bee pronouncer. I had no idea it would be her. She introduced herself, Robbie, me, and the three judges.

She went over all the rules for the competition. Then she explained how the procedures were to be followed by those in the audience. She informed them the auditorium was to be quiet when someone on the stage spoke, including her, and especially the contestants, Robbie and me.

When she had finished, she looked in our direction and said, "Are you ready?" We both nodded to indicate we were. The spelling bee began. My name was the first to be called. I stood up, took a breath, and proceeded to stand at the podium. Because of my height, I had to stand on a stoop placed at the podium.

My first word was "determination." I thought, "That's an easy one."

The more words called out, the longer and harder they became. I made sure to face the judges as I spelled my words. Several times, I requested for the pronouncer to repeat the word and sometimes to use it in a sentence. I made sure I always said the word before and after I spelled it. I was not going to be disqualified for failing to do so.

During our coaching period, I learned that the rules for the final round are different from the earlier competitions before becoming a finalist. Robbie and I had the same spelling bee coach, who had given us a copy of those rules in our study package. They read as follows:

FINAL ROUND GROUND RULES

When only two students are left in the competition, the rules of the game change slightly. If the first student misspells a word, the second student must spell it correctly and must also spell the next word on the list correctly to win the spelling bee. If the second student fails to spell the first word correctly, a new word is given to the first student to spell. If the second student fails to spell the second word correctly, the first student has a chance to spell it. The spelling bee ends when a student successfully spells both words.

Only a couple more rounds to go. After spelling my 39th word, I heard someone shout, "Oh no!"

The pronouncer reminded the audience the room must remain quiet except for the individual speaking on stage. Then she looked over at me and said, "I'm sorry, Affinity, but that is incorrect." I had no idea I had misspelled continent. That was an easy word too. I guess I must have still been nervous because I had spelled it with "e" and not "i." The pronouncer then called Robbie back to the podium. He had to spell the same word, and he got it right. Then the pronouncer called out his second word, "lattice." This was it. If Robbie spelled that word correctly, it would be over for me. He would remain the champion for another year.

I lowered my head and quietly whispered a prayer. "God, I don't want to wish anything bad for Robbie, but you know how hard I've studied for this moment. Please, let me win this championship."

As I was about to accept that Robbie might be the better speller, he misspelled his second word, "lattice." That word was a dead giveaway, and he got it wrong. He spelled it as "lettuce." I couldn't understand why he didn't ask the pronouncer to say it in a sentence.

He missed it, and I was so glad he did. I had another chance.

This time, the pronouncer was talking to Robbie when she said, "I'm sorry, Robbie. That was incorrect. Please return to your seat."

I instantly felt sad for Robbie. As he returned to his seat, he looked down and avoided looking at me.

"Affinity, please step to the podium," called the pronouncer. I was still thinking about Robbie when I heard my name being called a second time.

"Affinity, please take the podium." I felt the intensity in the room as I stood up and began walking toward the front of the stage. It felt like the more steps I took toward the podium, the farther it moved away.

That was the longest walk I had ever had to make. Waiting for permission to begin, I looked down at Kaaya. She smiled and gave me another thumbs-up. "Lattice," said the pronouncer. I looked at the judges, then proceeded to spell the word Robbie had missed.

"Lattice, L-a-t-t-i-c-e, lattice." I had listened carefully and clearly made the distinction in the sounds between the two words, just like Kaaya had taught me to do.

I heard the words, "That is correct. Your second word is camouflage."

The auditorium was eerily quiet. I asked the pronouncer to repeat the word and use it in a sentence. The word was repeated and then used in a sentence. Briefly, I closed my eyes, took a deep breath, then quietly whispered to myself, *you got this.* I opened my eyes and looked directly at the judges. I said the word, listening carefully to each letter sound I made.

I began spelling it. "C-a-m-o-u-f-l-a…" I paused. The room was very quiet. I finished by calling out the remaining letters, "g" and "e." The words I heard next were, "That is correct!" I jumped up and shouted. People began to applaud across the auditorium. I was getting a standing ovation. I won! I looked down at Kaaya and could see she was happy for me. We smiled at each other, and she again gave me her famous thumbs-up. I could see her lips moving, "You did it."

Yes! I had done it! I won the Spring Spelling Bee. I was the new champion and felt on top of the world.

Mrs. Boyd came towards me with the winner's trophy in her hand. She held it and said, "This is for you." Initially, I was reluctant to reach for it, fearing I would drop it to the floor. That thing was big and looked very heavy. She looked down at me and said, "Congratulations, Affinity. I could not be prouder to have you as one of my students."

As I reached for my trophy, I saw mom enter the stage. She gave me a big hug and said, "This is the best birthday present ever. Congratulations, Affinity."

I told my mom, "Sometimes when I have a bad day, I tell you, 'This was the worst day of my life.' Well, Mom, today is not that day because it is the absolute best day of my life."

Then, my mom asked, "We both have something to celebrate today. Don't we?"

"Yes, we do," I answered happily." Kaaya joined us on the stage. I knew at that moment I could not have had a better friend than she. I hugged my friend and thanked her for encouraging me to take on this challenge.

Mrs. Boyd and I walked back to our classroom when it was over. When we arrived, there was a big surprise waiting for me. Mrs. Boyd's teacher's aide had decorated our classroom with a big sign that read: "Congratulations, Affinity." It's like they already knew I was going to win today. Was it because they saw I believed in myself?

In the rear of the room was a table covered with various delicacies: cupcakes, cookies, and a whole lot more. I was so on top of the clouds, figuratively, I didn't notice my mom standing by the window. I thought she had left. I walked over to her, this time with tears in my eyes, and said, "Mom, I can't believe this is all for me."

"Yes, it is. Being a winner does make you feel good." She visited for a few minutes before grabbing one of the cupcakes and proceeded to leave my classroom.

Mom thanked Mrs. Boyd, waving back as she exited the room. She took the trophy with her so I would not accidentally damage it on my way home from school. When I got home, Dad was already there. He had left work early to take us out to dinner to celebrate Mom's birthday. We all now had reasons to celebrate each other: Mom's birthday, Dad's new job, and me, the new Spelling Bee Champion. Dad walked over and gave me a smile and a big hug.

"I am so proud of you, my little heart girl. I had no doubt you would bring home that beautiful trophy."

I responded, "I will be at a new school next year. So, I can be like my friend Kaaya was to me this year. I can help another kid learn to enjoy reading, so they can become a winner, like me."

"HG, that sounds like a great idea. It is always good to pass kindness forward," Mom replied supportively. "Today, you proved that enough is never enough until you have given it your best."

Now to you, my Peek-in-a-Book reader, believe you can. Don't ever stop trying. You could someday be the one taking home the big trophy!

Brendalyn J

Special Acknowledgments

To my daughters, Kendra and Latrell, and my grandchildren, Chase and Ava, I love you.

To Marie, thanks for all you did to bless me in this endeavor.

Thanks to Lisa M. Butler for designing my custom author caricature.

Thanks to my niece Renita and her team at Mynd Matters Publishing for bringing my vision to life.

Thanks to my cousin Thelma Lou and my family, I appreciate your continued love and support!

CPSIA information can be obtained
at www.ICGtesting.com
Printed in the USA
BVHW021612300323
661462BV00013B/45

9 781957 092614